Nicholas Glover

Teisha N. Glover

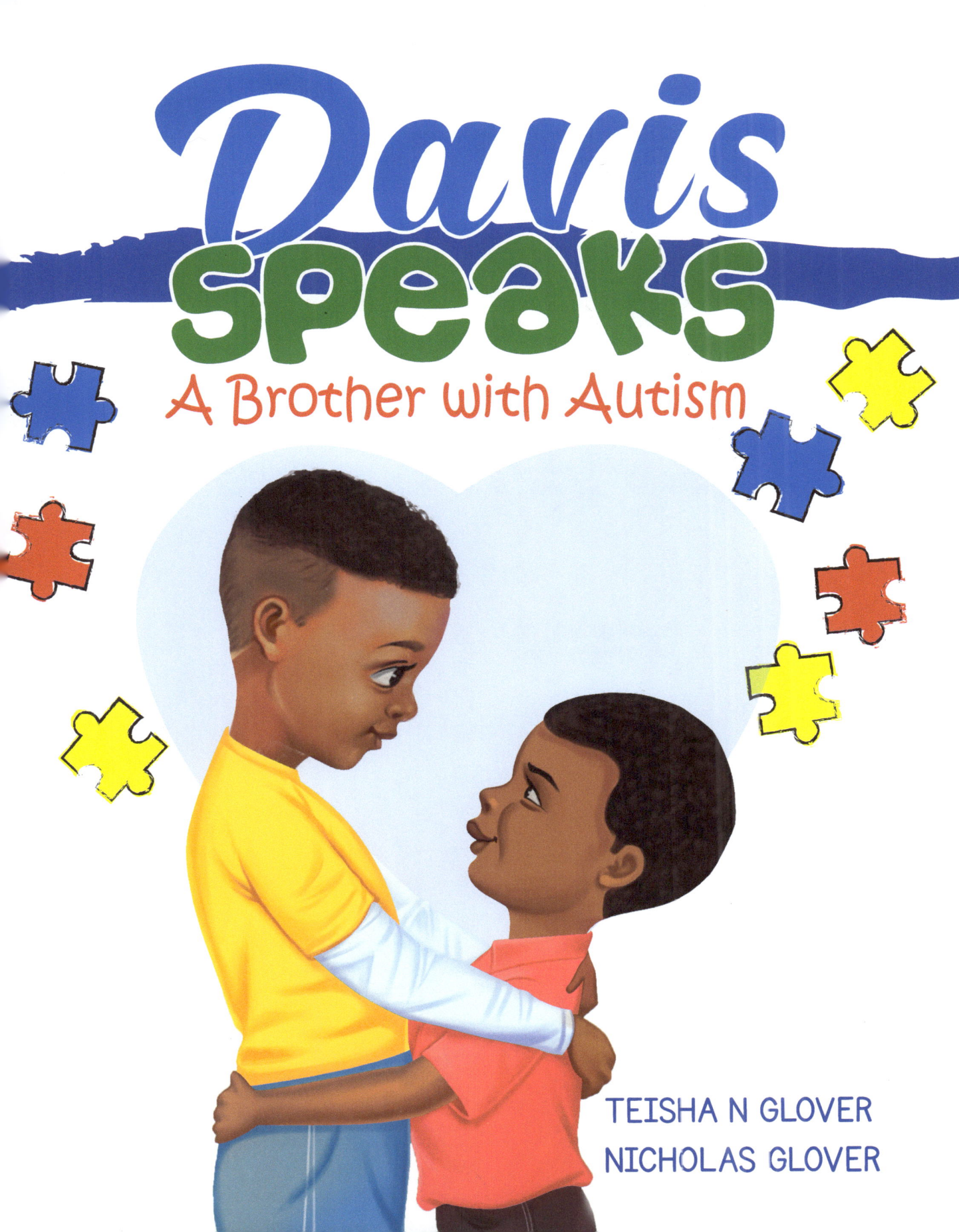

Davis Speaks—A Brother with Autism
Published by Exceeding Abundance Books

Copyright © 2020 by Teisha N Glover

Written by Teisha N Glover, Nicholas Glover

All rights reserved. No part of this publication may be reproduced, stored in a retrieval system or transmitted in any form by any means without the prior permission of the publishers and copyright owner or author.

ISBN: 978-1-7360316-0-5 (Paperback)
978-1-7360316-1-2 (Hardcover)

Text © 2020 Teisha N Glover
Illustration © 2020 Teisha N Glover
Layout and design © 2020 Teisha N Glover
Illustrations by Rajiv Kumar

To my Coauthor

You are the best big brother in the world.
You are gentle and strong, sensitive and bold, exceptional and humble.
Keep shining. I love you.

To my Baby Boy

You are a miracle.
You are smart and adventuresome, funny and courageous, sweet and loving.
You make my heart smile. I love you.

Nicholas, a friendly child, sometimes felt all alone, because he was the only little boy in his home. One day Nicholas got the most exciting news from his mother. In just a few months, he'd be a big brother.

"I'll have a best friend always by my side!"

And then the big day came,
Baby Davis arrived!

"When he is bigger, we will have so much fun riding bikes, playing catch, and running in the sun." Everyday Nicholas tried to teach Davis something new. He understood that's what big brothers were supposed to do.

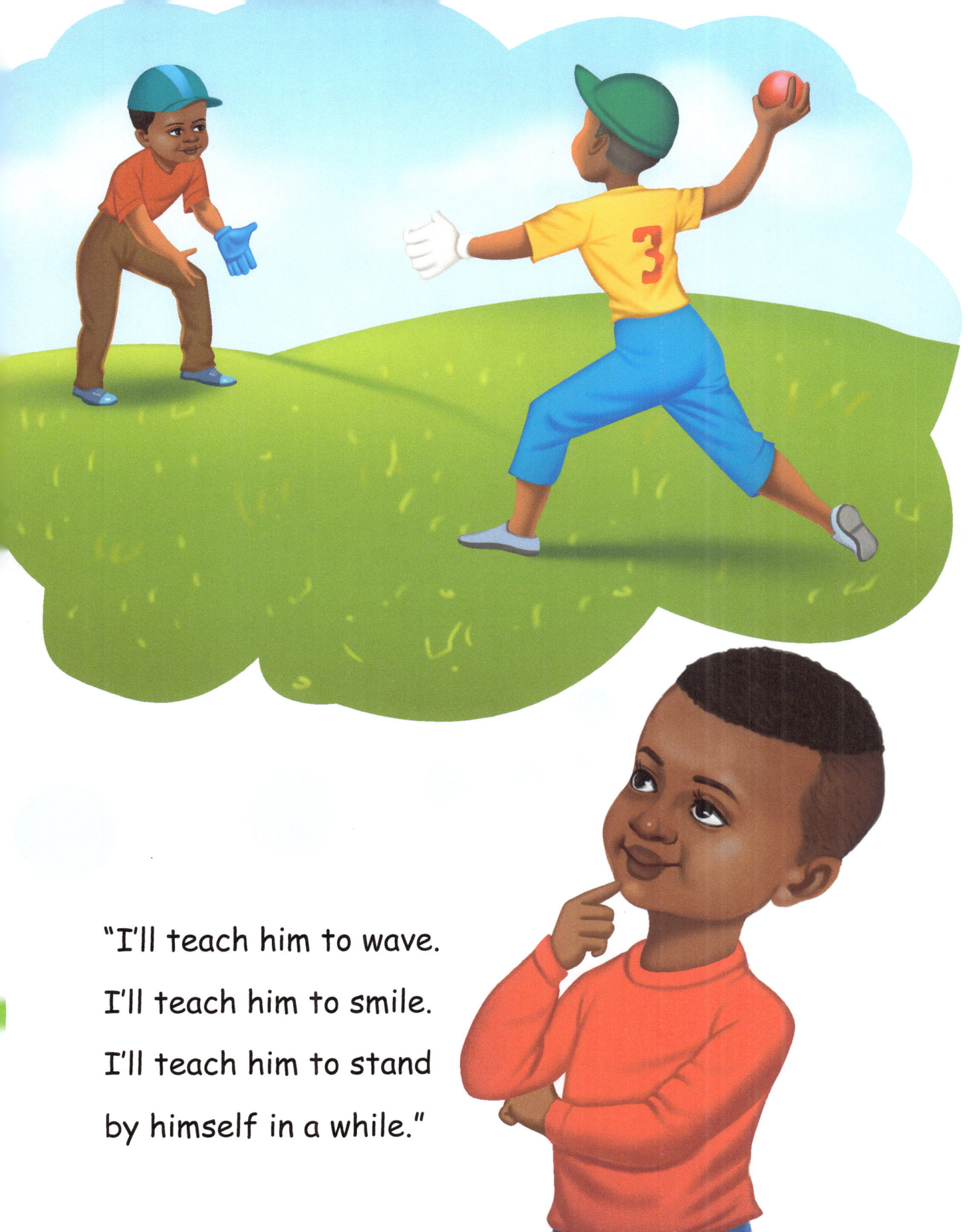

"I'll teach him to wave.
I'll teach him to smile.
I'll teach him to stand
by himself in a while."

But Davis didn't smile. Davis didn't even wave.

His doctor said, "Davis is developmentally delayed."

This was not expected. It was not in the plan, so Davis saw therapists to help him understand.

With help from big brother, Davis learned how to walk, and Nicholas was sure that he'd teach him to talk.

Davis learned sign language and to use cue cards. Little Davis was trying so very hard, but not a word did he utter as his big brother wished. Then, he was referred to another specialist.

The psychologist said, "Autism is the diagnosis.

His communication is different. I'm sure that you've noticed."

Autism meant that the family was extra prepared for a fearless little boy who tried anything he dared, but everyday activities were unpredictable.

Supermarket shopping would become a spectacle.

The people, the bright lights, the noise was all too much, and out of nowhere Davis would make a big fuss. He'd cover his ears. He'd chew on his shirt.

He'd squint his eyes as though the light even hurt.

He'd cry. He'd kick. He'd yell and scream.

Nicholas would be embarrassed by the scene, but Nicholas understood, Davis had no control. He'd been having meltdowns since he was two years old.

One day, Davis had the worst meltdown that he'd ever had. People stared and pointed as if he was just being bad. Nicholas was hurt by their attempt to cause shame. Couldn't they see that his brother was in pain? Nicholas hugged Davis closely and felt his heart beat. "Breathe. Breathe. Breathe, little brother. You're safe with me."

While some people only noticed the spectacle, Nicholas knew that his brother was exceptional. On the trampoline, no one could jump higher, a feat that Nicholas did admire.

He'd put Nicholas's trains in a perfect line, intensely focused the entire time.

He could climb trees to amazing heights. Then relax on the branches without a fright.

Thinking of his talents compelled Nicholas to sa

"I love you, Davis, and all your special ways."

When he looked into his eyes, there was no doubt, he knew, his little brother Davis was saying, "I love you too."

CPSIA information can be obtained
at www.ICGtesting.com
Printed in the USA
LVHW072220090821
694929LV00004B/49